ICKY, STICKY GLOOP

Written by Morgan Matthews
Illustrated by Yvonne Victor

Troll Associates

Library of Congress Cataloging in Publication Data

Matthews, Morgan.
 Icky, sticky gloop.

 Summary: In his desire to be an inventor, Benjamin
Franklin Bunny creates an icky, sticky mess called gloop.
 [1. Rabbits—Fiction. 2. Inventions—Fiction]
I. Victor, Yvonne, ill. II. Title.
PZ7.M43425Ic 1986 [E] 85-14013
ISBN 0-8167-0616-6 (lib. bdg.)
ISBN 0-8167-0617-4 (pbk.)

ICKY, STICKY GLOOP

Gloop? What is Gloop?
Gloop is icky! Gloop is sticky!
What an icky, sticky experiment
Gloop was!

Who invented Gloop? Benjamin
Franklin Bunny invented Gloop.
Benjamin Franklin was a
famous inventor. He invented
a lot of wonderful things.
Little Benjamin Bunny wanted
to be a famous inventor, too.

Little Benjamin liked to experiment. He liked to invent things. But Benjamin's experiments did not always work out the way they were supposed to!

Mrs. Bunny did not always like
Benjamin's experiments. For
instance, one day Benjamin
decided to experiment with
bubbles. He experimented in the
house. Oh, what an experiment!

There were bubbles here! There were bubbles there! Bubbles, bubbles were everywhere. "No more experiments in the house," said Mrs. Bunny.

Mr. Bunny did not always like
Benjamin's inventions, either.
Benjamin invented a new chair.
The new chair looked good.
Mr. Bunny sat in the new chair.
KA-BOOM! No more chair!
"What an invention!" cried
Mr. Bunny.
Poor little Benjamin! He wanted
to invent something useful. He
wanted to be like Benjamin
Franklin. What could he invent?

Benjamin looked at the broken
chair. He looked at his dog.
"That chair could use some
glue," Benjamin said.
His dog barked.

"Glue?" said Benjamin, and a strange look came upon his face. "I know what to do!" said Benjamin. "I will invent a new glue."

Away ran Benjamin Franklin
Bunny. Away ran the little dog.
Away they went to experiment.
Benjamin gathered things for his
experiment. He got special sticky
things. Sticky things are good
for making glue—and glue that
sticks is very useful.

"What good stuff," Benjamin said. "I have gooey melted marshmallows. I have maple syrup and honey. This stuff is the stickiest!"
Benjamin's dog barked.

"My glue will be special,"
Benjamin said. "Melted
marshmallows are sticky. Maple
syrup is sticky, too. Honey is
very sticky. What good glue this
will make."

Benjamin looked at the sticky
stuff.
"Now to experiment," he said.
He mixed melted marshmallows
with maple syrup. He mixed
that with honey. Benjamin
Franklin Bunny mixed up his
special glue.

Benjamin mixed and mixed.
ICK! What a mess! Benjamin
touched the messy mixture.
"It is certainly sticky," Benjamin
said. "But I want it stickier.
I know what to do!"
Benjamin gathered more sticky
things. He got jam. Jam is
sticky. He got bubble gum.
Bubble gum is sticky. And he
got something special. He called
the special something "X."

"This experiment is getting good," said Benjamin.
In went the jam. In went the bubble gum. In went "X."
Benjamin mixed it up.

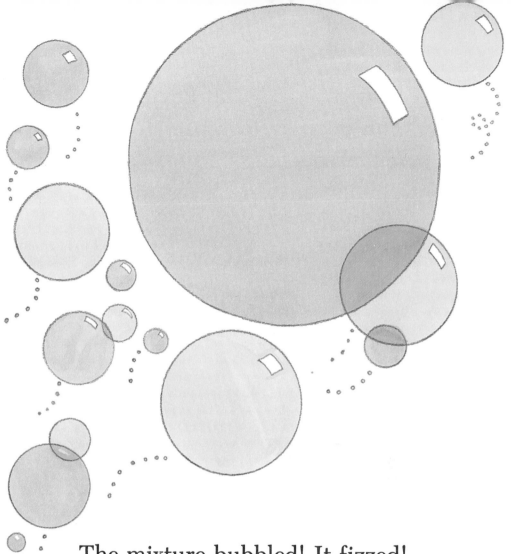

The mixture bubbled! It fizzed!
It fizzed and bubbled! The more
it fizzed, the bigger it got.
Oh, how it fizzed! FIZZ!
FIZZ! FIZZ!

"How strange," said Benjamin.
"This does not look like glue."
He looked at the fizzing,
bubbling mixture. What did it
look like?
Benjamin said, "It looks like
Gloop!"

GLOOP? Icky, sticky Gloop it was! The Gloop bubbled and fizzed. It fizzed and bubbled. It got bigger and bigger.

FIZZ! FIZZ! FIZZ!
"What a big bubble!" cried
Benjamin. "What an experiment!
What an invention!"
Benjamin touched the bubble.
KA-BOOM! No more bubble!
What an icky mess. Gloop here!
Gloop there! Gloop everywhere!

Gloop was on the house. Gloop
was on the dog. Gloop was on
Benjamin.
"Help!" cried Benjamin. "Help!
I am stuck!"

Out of the house ran Mrs.
Bunny. She looked at the mess.
"Benjamin!" she called.
"What happened? What is this
strange stuff?"
Up to the little bunny she ran.

"It is Gloop," cried Benjamin.
"Gloop?" said Mrs. Bunny.
"What is that?"
Mrs. Bunny touched Benjamin.
She touched the Gloop. Poor
Mrs. Bunny.

"Ick!" Mrs. Bunny cried.
"Gloop is sticky. I am stuck.
We are stuck together. How do
we get unstuck?"
"I do not know," Benjamin said.
"Call for help," said Mrs. Bunny.

"Help!" called Benjamin.
"Help! Help!" cried Mrs. Bunny.

Benjamin's dog wanted to help.
He barked and barked. Up to
Mrs. Bunny he ran. The dog
touched the Gloop. That was a
big mistake!
"Help!" called Benjamin.
"Help! Help!" cried Mrs. Bunny.
"Woof! Woof!" said the dog.
Out of the house ran Mr. Bunny.

Mr. Bunny looked at the mess.
He looked at the dog stuck to
Mrs. Bunny. Then he looked at
Benjamin.
"Another experiment," he cried.
"What happened? What is this
stuff?"

"It is icky, sticky Gloop," said
Mrs. Bunny.
"Gloop?" said Mr. Bunny.
"What is that?"
He went up to Benjamin.

"Do not touch the Gloop!" cried
Benjamin.
But it was too late. Mr. Bunny
did touch the Gloop. And what
happened? He got stuck, too.
Poor Mr. Bunny!

"Help! I am stuck," Mr. Bunny
cried. "I cannot get unstuck.
How did you make this sticky
stuff?"
"I mixed melted marshmallows
and honey," said Benjamin.
"I used maple syrup and jam.
Then I mixed in bubble gum and
something called 'X.' It made
good glue. Sticky glue is useful."

Mr. and Mrs. Bunny looked at
Benjamin.
"This is useful?" asked Mr.
Bunny.

"Call for help," Mrs. Bunny
cried.
"Help! Help!" Benjamin called.

The mailmouse was at the
Bunny house. He had the mail.
"What is that?" said the mouse.
"Is someone calling for help?"
Around the house ran the
mailmouse.

38

The mailmouse touched the
Gloop.
"Oh no," said Mr. Bunny.
"Now you are stuck, too."
The mailmouse looked at the
Gloop.
"Stuck?" he said. "Who is
stuck?"

The mailmouse wanted to get
unstuck. He tried and tried.
But he could not. Out flew the
mail from his sack. Mail stuck
here. Mail stuck there. Mail
stuck everywhere. What a mess!

KA-BOOM!
"What is that?" said Mr. Bunny.
Benjamin said, "I do not know."
KA-BOOM!
Mr. Bunny looked up.
"Rain," he said. "It is going to rain."

"Oh no," said Mrs. Bunny.
"We cannot go in the house.
We are stuck out here. It will
rain on us."

KA-BOOM! Rain it did.
Oh, how it rained! It rained
on everyone and everything.
It rained all over the Gloop.

Fizz! Fizz! Fizz!
"Look!" cried Benjamin.
"The Gloop is melting. Rain
melts Gloop. We are getting
unstuck!"

Fizz! Fizz! Fizz! The Gloop
bubbled and fizzed. The rain
melted all the Gloop. Benjamin
got unstuck. Mr. Bunny got
unstuck. Mrs. Bunny got
unstuck. The mailmouse and the
dog got unstuck.

"Good," said Mr. Bunny. "No
more Gloop. No more icky,
sticky mess."
He looked at Benjamin.
Benjamin was looking at the
mail in the rain. It was soaked.
Benjamin Franklin Bunny's face
got that strange look. Benjamin's
dog barked.
"Rain?" said Benjamin. "Mail?"
"I will invent a way to keep
mail dry."

Away ran Benjamin. Away ran
his dog.
"Uh-oh," said Mr. Bunny to Mrs.
Bunny. "Here we go again."